I0783577

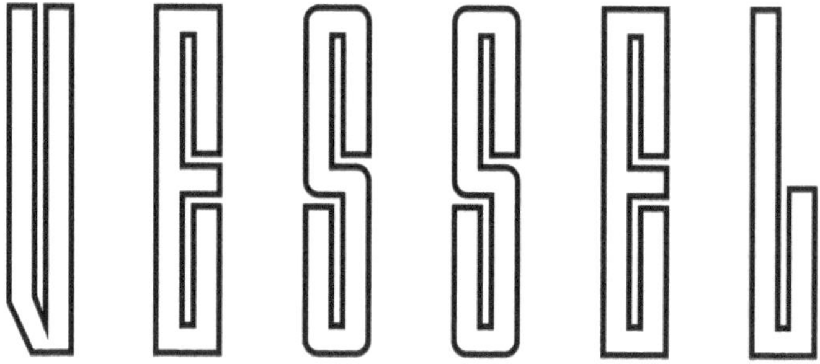

VESSEL

ANDREW REICHARD

Solum Literary Press
Mesa, AZ

Cover art by Sarah Christolni
Cover and Interior Design by Sarah Christolini

ISBN 979-8-9879514-0-8

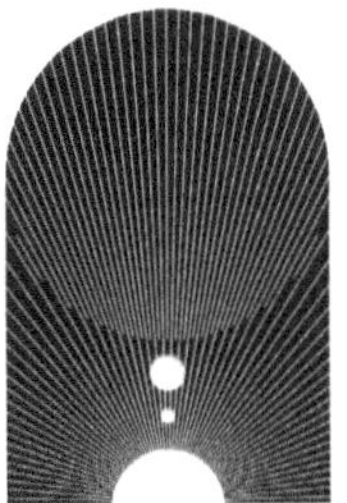

Solum Literary Press
2055 E Hampton Ave, 235
Mesa, AZ 85204
(480) 371-9053
info@solumpress.com

To my sons, Elliott and Beckett, who, as infants, slept best nestled beside me on the couch as I wrote this, the painting on the wall above us.

Vessel

As if entering a dream, Tennar drifted into a childhood memory. It was a memory of the painting in his father's house on Gaia: he thought this almost before the words made sense to him — the memory, which was not quite anything (painting or house) tangled up in the dream, which was both memory and the sensation of sudden remembrance at once. He had been making his way along the hangar of the spaceship, Vessel, then to feel a terrific pressure as though gravity had suddenly been inflicted upon him: an impression of blue depth, of deepness; and he thought of the painting.

Pausing there in the center of the open area, one steadying hand on the push net, Tennar hung weightless, more or less motionless, gazing past his feet along the curvature of the ship's circumferential passage. But he didn't see the walls or the node lights along its outer surface or the series of doors along the center of the wall of its inner surface. It was as if that particular breed of blue called 'deep' had cascaded out of its canvas border and flooded him, flooded Vessel itself, many billions of lightyears distant from home though he was.

Tennar was frustrated, then, when, after such a powerful sensation, and from nowhere, he found himself unable to recreate the image of the full painting. He felt he should have been able to piece it together as a puzzle, in a manner that suggested its complete form, even if there remained gaps. He thought he should have been able to 'see' it. The deep dash of blue in his mind had been a representation of water, he thought, reasonably, but there had been so much more to the painting than this formless hue. He remembered that it had nearly filled one wall of his father's living room . . .

(It wasn't until later that Tennar would come to recall — as suddenly as the recollection of the painting itself — that his father used to hold him up in front of this painting, had probably done this many times. And, in that way, Tennar had once come to know it: the painting that he had forgotten until just then, on his way to the navigation center on Vessel so many subjective years later.)

But at that first flash of dreamlike memory — the blue, the deepness, the *feeling* of deepness, both gentle and burdensome — he knew with absolute certainty that he had loved this painting. And he wished he could have seen it again.

~

When he arrived in the navigation node, he was greeted by the gradual illumination of its soft white light — the circuitry and wiring that powered the computers becoming visible as furrows and deltas all throughout the semitransparent walls like a massive, subterranean ant nest.

There was a chair built into the center of the room, but he'd never strapped himself into it, preferring to pause by the A/M panel and simply cue the report from there. Tennar wasn't a pilot. The austere black chair had been one of their concessions to the man they'd assumed he was. And if he'd once been that man on Gaia, he'd quickly become someone else the moment he'd left the Solar orbit, never to return.

Touching the A/M panel, he was informed that the ship had made two superlight relocations in the last 48 hours. Unusual, but not remarkable. Information that he knew he might simply accept, his mind still partially on the partial memory of the painting. He wasn't an engineer or a technician and had limited control over Vessel's trajectory in any case.

Schematics appeared on the wall panels around him, hiding the busy circuitry. Names and proximities of the region's stars and whatever bodies of matter drifted close enough to the range of illumination to be picked up by the sensors — names that were made up mostly of numbers, just as their proximities were numbers: computer-generated identifications no different than those found on barcodes in a supermarket. Where he was now fell well outside the farthest reaches of any Gaian telescopes and had for a long time. The distances no longer meant anything to him. He would have had to be a mathematician to understand them, and he wasn't that either.

A small smile came to Tennar's lips, one that defined the inevitable diminishment of awe he was capable of feeling for infinite distances and absurdly large numbers. 60 billion lightyears. 200 billion lightyears. 30 trillion . . . well beyond the horizon of what had once been called the Observable Universe. Just as it was useless to describe superlight relocation capability in terms of *speed*, it was meaningless to talk of the Universal Space in terms of *size*. Eventually, vastness became a concern of God's, and space itself a matter of the spirit.

But neither was he a priest, though he could appreciate the cave- or pillar-dwelling ascetics of old and mystical Christianities. Men who wandered off into the mountains wearing rags and chewing the hairs of their beards. Whoever he'd once been on Gaia, Tennar had become someone who believed — or, anyway, told himself he believed — that the essence of human sublimeness lay in solitude. Though he'd long left behind the days that he felt himself approaching what he once might have called an apotheosis. Increasingly, the only thing he thought he had was a curated gallery of memories in which he was not the curator. And the only thing he thought he might yet accomplish in the time he had left was to disclose them to himself, his own memories.

~

Tennar reasoned that this sentiment — the final organization or alignment of his memories in the context of the possible universe — was still in keeping with his initial purpose, which was to be a capsule of knowledge in the endless corridors of open space and theoretical emptiness. He preferred the more literal word 'capsule' to any metaphysical/humanistic term, such as 'beacon' or 'light.' Earth — which he had decided to call Gaia (since there was no one here to argue with him) — had a still loftier title for what his purpose was. So lofty that it was impossible he could be anything other than doomed.

But he'd known this! There was nowhere, actually, to go. No destinations. Every Earth-like world within the horizon of visible space had already been analyzed by more qualified men and women than he. None

4

of these new earths met all the requirements of a ready habitat for human-ity's growth. And no life forms, microscopic or otherwise. Of course, in-genuity and appalling amounts of time and money could put them on track to terraform —— but Tennar had left behind these schemes of expansion and fortune. He was only a capsule. A kind of living Voyager Record.

"If any alien ever asks, I know that Beatles song that Sagan's team couldn't get the rights to," he said aloud.

The ship's voice command sensors blinked at him from the wall panel, unable to recognize a command in his words.

He waved off the query light the way he might have shooed a fire-fly from his face in a Gaian dusk. It occurred to him to sing the Beatles song to himself, but then maybe he couldn't recall the lyrics anyhow. He knew one, two lines, a sad melody, and he felt a kind of maudlin dreari-ness about the bland fact of the words and their fleeting fame. It occurred to him, briefly, to place the song in history: which war had been going on when it was written?

In sudden annoyance, Tennar shut off the schematic displays and slung himself from the navigation node, nearly colliding with the chair in the center. The ship's illumination lit up the walls of his passage, creating shapes like puzzle pieces that brightened swiftly and then faded away again behind him. At the door, he punched the A/M panel to open it, since no doors would open in the ship without a tactile order from him first, and he threw himself spinning into the open area of its orbital bay where all the doors to all the various compartments of his world resided.

The fact was that his old world, its history and what might be called its events, seemed to him like nothing more these days than a grand mythology. Homeric in its propensity for long lists of otherwise forgotten names attached to shiny epithets. Only a few of his own memories felt acutely real.

But memory had no limits and was often indistinguishable from imagination. These were the circles of his mind. The basic elements of all his ideas and his reality were restlessness and loneliness: two elements, as with the beguilingly simplistic molecular makeup of water — one part restlessness and two parts loneliness, perhaps — fused together: R_2L might have been the chemical formula of his mind. This thought itself was a perfect example of that makeup! Tennar refused to put his thoughts in their place, to arrange them into a hierarchy of importance or relevance. The admittedly weak metaphor comparing the molecular structure of water with the condition of his thoughts was no less relevant to him than the fact that Vessel had made two superlight relocations in the last 48 hours, neither of which were any more or less important than the fact that 'A/M' was an acronym for the stupidly redundant *actual/material* — another panel against which he mashed his thumb to open another door to another compartment of the ship.

~

Tennar wanted to remember the painting in his father's house clearly, vividly, he wanted to *look at it*. He thought he was capable of this. But it would require the proper application and focus, having been from so long ago, in another time.

The corridor that led to the part of the ship he was entering curved down sharply like the mouth of a tunnel. Tennar propelled himself at the ceiling just above the corridor joint and, twisting in midair, positioned himself so that his feet were ready to spring out just before he collided with the wall of moving lights and propel his body from that contact with what had been the ceiling (and was now the floor) into the mouth of what had been the tunnel (and was now the next segment of upright path). He put his hands out to push himself away from the walls, but his self-calibration had been accurate enough, and he caught himself against the padding around the inner door and kicked the A/M panel by his feet. Vessel's lights responded in a brightening runway formation down the tube he'd just thrown himself, and when the light reached the door, the door opened.

Inside was his bunk as well as the few personal affects that he'd decided before he left Gaia he couldn't live without — things which he no longer noticed nor assigned any importance to. The bunk was important for sleeping. Only in it, strapped down to it, was he able to maintain an appropriately deep sleep. When he slept in the open orbital hangar, which had become a bad habit lately, he had to wear a helmet, and his rest was broken up by soft collisions with the walls. Tennar needed immobility now. Deep, REMful sleep, waking up from which he might find himself able to drift back into certain aspects of his memory that his mind must have been unconsciously working out.

The memory of the painting had come to him suddenly, for no apparent reason. His subconscious thinking had hoisted him up to eye-level with it for a flashing instant before it was gone again. A feeling of perfect sublimeness: an image from his earliest memories that was disassociated from any events that could have been in any way useful in the 'summary' of his life or his station in respect to the world. It was simply a painting that he had once been attracted to, borne up from the deepest waters of his inner self where only a few particles of light penetrated …

But he couldn't sleep. He lay tolerantly for a long time on his back with one strap over his chest and the other over his thighs, mashing his eyelids together because they didn't want to stay closed.

~

It was not a logical issue for Tennar that he had attached a certain amount of mysticism to this deep blue memory of the painting. He wasn't a devotee of logic, necessarily, and he had decided that it was for this reason that he'd been chosen for this journey, and it was for this reason that he'd accepted.

He wasn't mad; he was simply a product of his time — a time that had been capable of producing something as grand and illogical as superlight relocation technology, which humanity had just as illogically assumed would make distance (the very concept of distance) obsolete. But the Universe had already made the concept of distance obsolete, and 60 trillion lightyears of *space* meant roughly the same thing as a single lightyear; and, though Vessel was doing its best, humanity (as exemplified by poor Tennar (Tennar thought to himself)) would never see, reach, know, intimate, etc., the edges, contours, or limitations of anything.

And it was for this reason that Tennar had entirely ceded control over Vessel's coordinates to the parliament of supercomputers that was Vessel's core. He'd done this a long time ago, even before they'd left their own galaxy behind, because he understood clearly that he had been chosen for this journey for his capacity to make that exact decision.

He'd known they'd wanted this from him. Though they'd never asked for it directly, they had been keen to remind him over and over that he was "a product of his time."

What was "his time", he wondered? It certainly wasn't this. This apparent stasis. This was a winding down. A riding irretrievably off into the light of far too many other suns, whose lights paradoxically appeared always to be dimming as he approached, as though they were powerless to do anything other than set.

The human race that he'd left behind had — out of a sense of desperation — attempted to sneak up on the ultimate mysteries of the Universe through a kind of reverse psychology: instead of rigid science and logic, they'd attacked the problem with a reckless sense of implausibility and open-sourced theories. And it had appeared to work! Born from this mindset was superlight relocation technology. Born from this mindset were people like Tennar —

Who now, finally, found himself convinced that the Universe — which had responded with its own reckless and illogical theories — had to have been the product of, was at the behest of, a willful designer. (He was convinced of this because it was far too narrow-mindedly logical to think otherwise.)

For the sake of simplicity, and, by that justification, because the title seemed incapable of objectifying the personhood (either by know-ability or unknowability) of its bearer, Tennar had decided to refer to this designer as God.

~

Having been unable to sleep when he'd wanted to, his thoughts turned idly to breaking things. There was one piece of equipment on the ship that he was always tempted to sabotage, and he had been since the beginning of his journey. This was the superlight system relay, which was situated in a compartment adjacent to the navigation node: a fragile-looking bell-shaped object in the center of its globular relay-enhancing compartment. It collected packets of data from Vessel's computers and dispersed them along something like the trajectory the ship had taken, using a reverse copy of the relocations to throw this data back at Gaia.

Since the presence of this compartment seemed to be against the basic character of Vessel's (and, by extension, Tennar's) mandate, Ten-nar had been assured of two things: the first being that this relay was not one-hundred-percent accurate, and some of the data would inevitably not be received by Gaian receptors; and the second was that the relay was fragile in the extreme and shouldn't be tampered with. He'd received a light and unconvincing scolding on this matter before leaving. Even being in the room with it, Tennar had been told, was a strain on its systems.

He was in the room with it now. Hovering just inside the doorway, gazing somewhat morosely at the object. Its pick-up sensors were flickering along the circumference of its base, making small grumbles: an attempt to adjust to the interruption of Tennar's presence, perhaps even to his body temperature.

"My very own forbidden tree," he said and was rewarded by an agitated redoubling of the flickering lights and the soft machine grumbles.

He couldn't remember if he'd said these words before, from this exact position. Tennar was aware that he had the tendency to repeat himself. He would sometimes drift for hours and hours languidly around the bay of the ship, repeating all the things he could remember having said in his life, especially the most embarrassing things. Doing this gave him a sense of extreme tranquility.

Tennar had, after all, his eccentricities. But by what reference point were his eccentricities to be considered eccentric? His only companions were Vessel and the memories within him. This little piece of equipment was his only connection to Gaia, and it was a one-way connection at that — this relay unit that was humanity's single hope of gaining anything back from Tennar's journey, any knowledge. It was almost as if they wanted him to break it. They'd certainly left the option up to him. Temptation built into the closed system of his life.

~

But his life wasn't a closed system. He had memories, and they were important to him. He had once cherished a certain type of literature whose readers' ears were meant to prick up at simple words like *memory* and *dream*, and the only reason he could think of to explain this bizarre short-cut through the space between a word and the material of significance was that both actual memories and actual dreams were themselves as distant from life as words were, and yet they still carried a sense of weightless magnitude in the human mind.

~

That he had thought of the memory of the painting in his father's house as coming to him in the form of a dream was not surprising to Tennar. What was surprising was the feeling of love he had had toward the painting.

While drifting slowly around the orbital rind of *Vessel*, in a fresh set of loose-fitting silicone clothes, he tried to decide where this sense of love came from and what it meant. The most obvious possibility was that it was an associative link to an unremembered period of his life that had been full of love. He couldn't have been older than two or three at the time, probably younger, and almost all of that time was entirely lost to him, as such an age was with most people. By the time Tennar was five, or maybe six, his parents had moved into the three-room apartment in which he had grown up. And what had become of the painting?

The second-likeliest reason for this feeling of love was that the painting — or the fleeting, dreamlike sensation he retained of the painting — was simply the only object in a vast sea of blankness. The fact that he had retained this singular object of memory from such an early age might not have been so much a simple trinket of reminiscence as a useful key to his own identity.

Realizing this gave Tennar a slight feeling of dismay. If his attraction to the memory of the painting was only an attraction to some touchstone of his self, then his solipsism went much deeper than he anticipated. Being so distant from the earth (which he couldn't even bring himself to call "Earth" anymore) that his interest in its affairs had dwindled was inevitable. But this level of rooted self-interest was something else. How was he to escape this?

He thought about his old friends and family little enough as it was. At first, Tennar had assumed this to be appropriate, since he knew he'd never see them again: a form of self-defense! But sometimes his perceived failure of empathy, even all the way 'out here,' worried him. What if he were eventually discovered by a technologically profound species of extraterrestrial who, in scanning his brain, concluded from their sample that the human race entire was a dangerous breed of alien devoid of compassion, and this caused them to target Gaia as a potential threat?

Obviously, this sort of run-off imagination was no surprise, considering how much solitary time he had on his hands. And his thoughts were always circular anyway: because of the concern for his own empathy, Tennar had once entertained the idea that he was indeed a *product*, not just of his time, but in the general sense. (But these delusions of androidhood had culminated only in an increased attempt to speak to Vessel "man to man," as he'd told it. Its response had been a soft, suffusive glow from all its nearby circuits, followed by darkness, and Tennar decided that he had offended it.) His final hope was that his empathetic concerns were, ultimately, a sign that he still had a soul.

~

But the third likeliest reason for his love of the painting was the least psychoanalytical and the one he liked the most: that the sensation of love he had toward the painting was itself a literal memory: something in his little mind at the age of about two or maybe three had caused him to love this painting then. And Tennar was suddenly certain that this love and the image of the painting itself was important to his present situation, somewhere in a distant plane of unknown space.

~

Tennar thought he might have been overthinking things. But he couldn't be sure! His thoughts had taken on the form of a jigsaw puzzle: an elaborate design carved into a simple form. Or, to reduce the metaphor to something too close at hand for comparison: his thoughts seemed to have become an imitation of Vessel, whose impossibly intricate and various softwares appeared to him sometimes trapped within this shell of a ship whose form — though not exactly simple — was easy to follow.

By now, he could have found his way to any compartment of the ship with his eyes closed, barely brushing against the light-riddled walls, as he was doing now. There were few enough places to go, anyway. Each door leading inward from the orbital bay along a pipework corridor to the compartment or node at its far end, each one containing its own function and purpose, separate from the others.

There was an organizational comfort to this, but Tennar couldn't ignore the two doors (one at either axis) that had always remained locked to him. And he couldn't ignore the fact that the ship itself (the circumference of which he spent a lot of time floating around in) was far larger than the compartments he had access to could account for. Either the locked doors led to a system of rooms that broke the rule the rest of the ship followed, or else there were vast areas of space *in between* the compartments and their constituent corridors.

With his eyes shut, he maneuvered himself by the web of the catch net on the outer wall. Sightless motion without resistance. Let go of the netting and float free, and he could imagine that there was no ship — that he was adrift in the void. The only container for his mind was his body, without which his mind would have been capable of drifting from one edge of the Universe to the other in the eternity it would take.

A soft white light that his eyes sensed shallowly from inside their lids. Light that was alive without the detection of actual motion, like the majestic spiral of a distant galaxy. He opened his eyes and saw the lights of Vessel's sensors around the first locked door. The sensors were responding to his presence; a complex system of scintillation that ran up and down the walls surrounding the door, the comparisons for which there was no end: the lights were like white blood cells responding to a virus in a body; they were like an overlapping heat map of many great migrations of birds; or like visible streams of data from all Vessels in all directions of space toward the surface of a knowledge-needing, knowledge-fearing world . . . there was no end. Tennar floated before the door, watching the lights, mesmerized, attempting to see in them the simile that was closest: what they were *actually* like. It was an impossible task. He didn't even know why Vessel responded this way to his proximity to the locked doors — whether it was a warning or something else. Perhaps the key to opening them was embedded in the pattern.

Tennar reached out and touched the door as he had many times before. He pushed. There was no A/M panel, so, technically, there wasn't even a 'keyhole.' Playfully, he knocked.

"Open sesame," he said. He also said, "Knock, and the door shall be opened unto you." After a moment, he said, "It's just you and me out here," directing his words to the light display that surged along the curvature of the wall. "So why don't we just open up to each other."

It was useless. Vessel was programmed to respond this way, and it couldn't respond any other way unless the protocols changed. Tennar, watching the continuing dance of lights, felt a growing unease as when a supposedly domesticated dog fails to settle its hackles after the initial greeting of a stranger is passed.

"Vessel," he said to Vessel. "Where are we going?" Tennar knew the answer to this already. For more reasons than one, it was pointless to ask. They would go as far as they could in a single basic direction. If there was anywhere to get to — if there were any limits at all — he and Vessel would come as close to it as humanly and/or mechanically possible.

~

Sometimes Tennar was mentally assaulted by a feeling of absolute certainty, but what he was certain about was never absolutely certain. He felt sometimes — without being capable of explaining how he arrived at the idea — that knowledge led *only* to liberation. Further and further liberations until all that was left was open space and freeform nothingness. A perfect void of knowing.

~

Drifting was his basic mode of movement, and Tennar pondered how this might be amplifying his unfortunate psyche. Put another way, the restless/lonely makeup of his thoughts might have been enhanced by this weightless drifting simply because he was unable to apply any physical pressure to the problems in his life. (Luckily, he had the A/M panels.) But had he been on Gaian ground, he might have found that walking, with the gravitational weight in his shoulders and joins, made his thoughts paradoxically swifter, more exuberant or agile.

But gravity wasn't the only consideration here! There was atmosphere: certain scents and pressures, interruptions. They — his thoughts — would have heavily depended on where in Gaia he was walking. And, on that stand, he would also have to take into account the massive variety of visual stimulants on his home planet. Here, within this atmosphere of recycled air, with little else to look at but metal walls and sensor lights, he might only have been capable of a limited number of ideas and creative memories.

Had he been on Gaia, remembering the painting with perfect clarity could have been a simple matter of stepping out on some beach and picking his way, with slouched shoulders, along the shoreline where he could actually *see* the deep blue …

If it had been possible for Tennar to stop in his tracks, he would have. What happened to him physically when the thought entered his consciousness was that he straightened suddenly, tipping him into a slow backwards tumble toward the ceiling of the bay. He didn't notice. His body was rigid and remained so. The moment he'd thought of the beach being a place that might help him stimulate the memory of the painting, he realized that he'd picked the wrong ecosystem. Though he knew there was water, Tennar felt sure it wasn't an ocean that was depicted in the painting, but a lake. A lake so isolated and so darkly pristine — surrounded by mist-laden mountains and large stones! — that it was possible Tennar had, at that impressionable young age of near infancy, seen in the painting an as yet unarticulatable sensation of solitude.

This excited him very much. He almost didn't catch himself before knocking his head against the plate metal ceiling. By a sort of accidental process of elimination, he'd expanded his mental image of the painting exponentially! He now had a mountain lake. But putting it so objectively left him disappointed with this revelation. It couldn't have been just a picture of a lake surrounded by mountains; it had left such a fissure in his mind.

Carefully, Tennar backtracked to his initial impression: the deep blueness of the painting. A blueness of such weight and depth that it felt eternal, even as, at this very second, eternity was being demonstrated to him. This was remarkable. No actual lake on any world could have expressed this sensation. It must have been that the painting (as Tennar's initial impression of it asserted) had something of the fantastical about it, that from its lines and colors arose a plane of impressions that was greater than the area of what objective description could resolve. The image of the things in the painting itself — lake and mountains — was only its center, its starting point; and it hadn't even been by these things that Tennar had found his way back to it.

Still, they must have been important. What had he seen in the painting that he could describe? Mountains along the background with the lake in the center and great grey boulders in the foreground and corners. This was it, undoubtedly. These facts of description beside the borderless mass of the painting's (or memory's) emotional weight were as dull to him as a recap of the 'events' of his life beside certain of its *total images*.

It occurred to him to think proudly of the painting as 'art', having as it did certain aesthetic qualities that must have made it so. But art, as an idea, was beside the point, as it always was when faced with an example of its actuality. Only critics thought like that, and he was the furthest thing from one of those, being (Tennar realized this) mostly without guile.

~

It was this guilelessness that allowed him, probably, to 'continue on' without falling into despair while Vessel made colossal calculation after colossal calculation, hurling them into new reaches of manifold emptiness with every relocation.

Five of which had been made in the last twenty-four hours, Tennar discovered the next time he consulted the navigation node's schematics.

"Five?" Tennar asked aloud, incredulous. "Even for you, Vessel, that's a bit rushed."

Systems of light crawled up the walls around him.

"As I understand it," he lectured, "superlight relocations are immensely hazardous, requiring great amounts of calculations to ensure that, when we relocate, we don't inadvertently overlap anything suitably large to — "

While he was talking, Vessel had relocated *again*. After only five minutes between the last one and now. He frowned at the cells of jittering lights on the walls, watching them. The sensors were strobing so swiftly that it was beginning to give him a headache. He tried to read the data streams on the wall, but Vessel's sensors were now flashing in chaotic forms behind it, and he couldn't see. They were too bright.

Keeping his eyes closed, he maneuvered toward the center of the room until he found the chair. At first, it didn't occur to him to sit in it; it was just something to cling to, like a sailor hugging the mast of a sinking ship in the middle of the ocean. Except that there was no similar drama of disaster. No alarms or automated warning voices. No detectable motion at all. Only the ecstatic lights of Vessel's sensors, against which Tennar held one hand as a shield across his eyes. He could tell, even through his fingers, that the sensors were all blinking at once now — rhythmically, impossibly bright, retina-slashing. He found it was possible to be physically pummeled by light.

Abandoning the captain's chair, Tennar propelled himself blindly through the door, along the corridor; he found the A/M panel and flung himself through the opening into the vaulting orbital openness of the bay — the huge empty space just inside the ship's hull. Even here, the bashing lights. An unfiltered whiteness. Radiant and mechanical. The flashing, each flash, must have corresponded with — represented — a single superlight relocation. He understood this, but it was impossible. Approximately, Vessel was relocating through the Universe at the rate of a resting heartbeat (his own was laboring).

But what was this new rate of motion capable of anyway but expanding humanity's impression of the unknowable? What could such expansions lead to? And what did it mean to him personally, except that Vessel's sudden charge was dangerous? But more dangerous than any single relocation? Vessel's movements had the appearance either of intensified purpose or else of the total disintegration of protocols: what would have been, in a human, insane recklessness. Its lights were frightening him more than the motion they represented.

Tennar opened his eyes and was greeted with the cerebral pain of being nearly blinded. He called out to Vessel to stop and was surprised to hear his own voice ring out clearly in the spaciousness, answered only by his own voice's echoes. The lights, of course, were silent, though their violence made this hard to believe. They had filled him with a panic of urgency, the need to do something. But there was nothing to do. He wanted gravity so that he would have the weight to run and escape from his terror. Weightlessness was a liberation that terrorized him. He flailed, unable to touch anything, having moved away from the door and lost his bearings. He didn't know how fast he was moving and could crash into any number of metal surfaces at any instant. He opened his eyes, briefly, snapping them shut again, opened them again in the pocket between flash and flash; he found the rhythm and maintained it, peeking out between explosions of light so that he managed to piece together a broken picture of where he was and where he was headed . . . to the far curvature of the outer wall and its catch net. He grasped a strand in his hand, eased his momentum across its surface: he hadn't been moving quickly, though he'd been sure he was hurtling like a comet.

It was at this point that immobility gripped him. For a long time, it took all the concentration he had to continue timing his eyes' openings to the breaks between Vessel's flashings. It was quiet enough in the chamber that he could hear the lids of his eyes clicking open; he was mesmerized by this. Somehow, the Universe and their involvement inside of it had ceased to matter the moment Vessel had fully committed itself to the extent of its powers of mobility. Tennar felt sure that even this manner of motion would be easily absorbed, and, without moving himself, he decided that there was still one thing he could do that would be of some use.

~

Before he set about doing it, though, he thought of the painting once more.

This wasn't a conscious thought process; it happened in the space of a flash of light and was likely caused by those same lights and his blinking between them, which had the effect of turning Tennar's entire world into a repeated mechanism of epiphany, so that his sight (which had decreased) and his intuitive perception (which had increased accordingly) were in the process of merging into equal halves: a condition that wasn't at all like a dream, but neither was it much like being awake.

It was in this half-state that he remembered something important about the painting — some smaller detail that he felt must have left a deep impression on him, that somehow felt connected to his current situation. The color of this detail was black or a very dark brown, and his mind placed it somewhere in the upper-middle of the full picture. Apart from that, he wasn't sure. It might have been a medium-sized hole in the canvas itself, but he was sure it was part of the painting, part of the intent . . . which might, then, have been the representation of a hole? A hole in the space between sky and water and mountain? Tennar was left with dwindling certainty. He had remembered this detail the way one catches sight of a shooting star at night, the resultant feeling of which was always immeasurable luck: the conditions were right, and his mind had happened to be aimed in that direction the moment the memory arrowed past. Except that his memory wasn't a bit of debris striking Gaia's atmosphere; it was a memory, and he must have retained something of it if he'd noticed it at all.

But by that point, Tennar had a headache coming on and couldn't concentrate. He had his bearings sufficiently calibrated. He shut his eyes and kept them closed.

~

In that manner he made his way to the compartment that contained the transmission relay. Tennar could keep his eyes closed the entire way if he moved slowly enough, though he occasionally found that a wall or an A/M panel was a little closer or farther away than he'd thought while approaching it.

Still, when he reached the compartment, it was with a feeling of exhilaration, as though he'd performed a great athletic feat. He felt dexterous and deft! And when Vessel opened the door, Tennar could tell that something about the room was different. There was no light beating against the walls of his eyelids. Within the relay compartment, Vessel's sensors held their peace.

Tennar shut out the still flashing corridor behind him and opened his eyes and looked around. Coming here had been a good idea, he decided. But what about what he'd come to do? The bell-shaped relay hung in the center of the circular room, the agitated lights of its sensors that registered his presence, an increased whirring from its air vents as though it were frightened.

Tennar laughed. The whirring and lights increased.

"Boo," said Tennar, somewhat sadistically. The whirring and lights increased to a pace and pattern that could have specified terror. He wondered what God would have said to his first couple had he returned to the Garden to find that they'd cut the Tree of Knowledge down instead of eaten of its fruit, to find them standing over its dead stump in mild bemusement. Was mankind even capable of sabotaging the rules in that extreme a manner? That he even wondered about it seemed a blasphemy, though he didn't exactly know why. If mankind wasn't capable of stepping that far out of bounds, was mankind truly free?

Baa! Freedom wasn't the issue at stake here, Tennar knew. It was like asking: if mankind wasn't capable of creating its own Universe in its own image, was mankind truly free? The question was preposterous, completely out of proportion. Certainly, there was some freedom: mankind was capable of asking preposterous questions! Given the choice between knowledge and obedience, mankind had the freedom to make the choice. That there were no third, fourth, fifth options — Tennar felt, magnanimously — was not God's problem. That the Tree of the Knowledge of Good and Evil had not also been the Tree of the Knowledge of the Exact Size of the Universe was also not God's problem.

As there was certainly some freedom, there was certainly some knowledge as a result of that freedom. But mankind — having become capable of making its own trees, fragile as they were — had reached the vertiginous state of wanting to know all knowledge, or at least of wanting to know the full extent of what remained to be known. It was this counter-logical mindset that had produced superlight relocation technology, had produced Tennar's own mission, had produced this particular piece of equipment, had produced the situation in which Tennar currently found himself: this choice that had been left with him.

Having gone through the process of these interesting thoughts, Tennar clapped his hands to rid himself of them, producing a shriek of mechanical jitters from the relay.

But then one more idea occurred to him…

~

He remembered that there was a readout beside the A/M panel that processed the human-readable information traveling from Vessel to the relay. Tennar could intercept this data to find out Vessel's rate of relocation from here without having to return to the navigation node. How convenient!

This was quickly confirmed, and it was as he expected: Vessel was relocating at the rate of its flashing, and its sensors were flashing (all of them but for those in the relay compartment) 65 times a minute, or just over once per second.

Tennar had already grown used to the idea of relocating that quickly. Nothing could surprise him anymore, and he felt only a rising annoyance that the sensors were also apparently flashing inside his personal quarters, that Vessel didn't have the decency to remember the human passenger's comfort! He shouted as much, the doomed relay muttering bleakly beside him.

It didn't do any good. Tennar glanced through the rest of the report, not understanding most of it anyway — except that something caught his attention just as he was about to turn away. According to this packet of data, the scanners of the surrounding space that Vessel was bounding through were repeatedly picking up . . . nothing. In fact, the ship's scanners had been picking up nothing ever since Vessel had started its manic stampede, and at every stop (which stops were just long enough for the scanners to confirm) this condition of the space around them was reconfirmed: total nothing. No nearby stars or supernovas or black holes. Not even the byproduct of any solar wind. The ship's scanners were not detecting a single atom, hydrogen or otherwise.

"That's not possible. The scanners must be broken," Tennar said to shield himself from the fact that he didn't believe they were broken. His words were completely mechanical and far behind his brain, which was thinking through its shock, that he'd found it: the edge, not just of known space, but of all space. Where he was now could not possibly be space since space was matter and energy and was not nothing. But this, assuming Vessel's analysis could be trusted, was Nothing.

~

Tennar's entire body hung slack, his feet a few inches above the floor where it sloped down to form the base of the sphere inside of which the transmission relay operated. It occurred to him to wonder if his heartrate was good, in that exact term. He shut his eyes again, this time out of a basically misguided desire to escape reality. Now, the lights were only inside of his eyelids, pulsing with the soft insistence of memories, moving, gradual and irrevocable, along an inner horizon to a point he couldn't follow.

~

If he'd had the imagination then to suggest to himself that he'd arrived at the commodious territory of Nothing for anything more than the sole purpose of disabling humanity's knowledge of Nothing, he might have wormed his way even further into a revelation of a kind. As it was, Tennar couldn't help but wonder why he'd bothered to make this journey in the first place — why anyone had thought the journey might be useful. It might have been a mercy to destroy the transmission and keep Gaia ignorant of what he'd found, but the mercy was a setup, like a doctor who spreads an illness in order to bandy the cure. But this example sounded too similar to a God who creates evil (or allowed it to exist — was there a practical difference?) in order to save us from it. Tennar was uncomfortable with this line of reasoning. He had to believe in processes. Without processes factoring into the end result, one could have said, "better if I'd stayed home, never woken up, never been born . . . " If Nothing was the Inherent State, then even nightmares were preferable. Nightmares from which one woke, or, as happened infrequently, within which one might remember that there was the assurance of waking.

So it was that, as Tennar maneuvered his way toward the transmission relay, he felt that what he was about to do was a simple act of mercy, like shaking the shoulders of someone clearly in the throes of a bad dream. Even though the dreamer might have been on the verge of some terrible revelation … Certain ignorances were still preferable, as humanity's very foremost lesson had shown.

~

But was there any mercy left over for him? He couldn't shake his own shoulders, wake himself up. The technicians who'd told Tennar that the relay equipment was fragile had not been lying. The moment his hands touched the bell-shaped surface, he felt something inside of it break. Its outputs gave a paltry bleat of noise and air, and its lights faded and went out.

At first, Tennar thought he was crying out of sentimental pity. He'd killed it with his bare hands — this thing that, machine though it was, had responded to his presence . . . So, then, these free-floating tears were only out of self-pity: Tennar had destroyed one of the only things on the ship that had in some manner communicated with him.

He didn't want to be here, filled with these theory-thoughts of matter and nothingness, evil and knowledge. It was all far, far too much to contain, especially while it contained him. He was tired of his solitude. He was tired of being impressed with his own loneliness. The banality of this feeling was rooted in the fact that there was no one to share his loneliness with. Except, possibly, for Vessel itself.

Before thumbing the A/M panel to open the door to the corridor, he shut his eyes, anticipating the blinding flashes of Vessel's excitement. But he could tell right away that the lights had ceased. Easing himself into the corridor, Tennar was filled with a strange fear: not existential, but immediate; the fear of a child preparing to peer under the bed in the dark.

"Vessel?" he called. He was inside of Vessel. He was calling for the computer to respond to him, but the computer was the ship, its software. No, that was inaccurate. He was inside of the ship; the computer was Vessel. But the ship was the computer, its hardware. So the ship was

Vessel, inside of which he called for it to respond to him. Which it had not.

"Vessel?" Tennar touched the A/M panel at the far end of the corridor, which opened the door to the open and empty hangar that orbited the entire diameter of the ship, where he was met with a consistent gloom. The only light came from the colorless nodes along its outer panels along the base of the push net. Did the absence of sensor-flashing mean that Vessel had stopped relocating?

He shoved lightly away from the mouth of the corridor, the door closing behind him, and put his momentum into a slow turn, studying the gloom around him. Absent of any obvious reference point, the thought came to him that space was the necessary medium with which to prove that light was boundless. This was quite hopeful! An idea he'd formulated for himself (based on the ideas of others, he couldn't remember who) at the outset of his journey. Light, of course, wasn't boundless, but anyway he didn't mean *light* in the literal sense.

This was a distraction, and annoying to him. There were things he needed to find out about his present situation. Such as: assuming Vessel had stopped relocating, did this mean that it had given up, died, or been distracted by a discovery?

These were the three anthropomorphic options that Tennar gave Vessel to cover up his absolute certainty that (regardless of whether one of those options approximated the truth) Vessel had stopped because it could no longer go on.

~

Faced with the problem of having found an ultimate endpoint, Tennar was also met with the opposite (and equal, he decided, for the comfort of symmetry) non-problem that nothing about his situation had changed. Nothing substantial, that is. It made no difference to Tennar that Vessel was no longer relocating, that the journey had ended. There had been nowhere to arrive at, and here he had arrived at nowhere.

The skin around his eyes felt tight and weary when he tried to smile to himself. All he had were memories and word games. Language was not equipped for the situation. Only a computer, like Vessel, could paint the surrounding emptiness with its sensors and describe what it saw there, which it was doing in the language of numbers and negation — a language from which he discovered, in the navigation node, he couldn't derive any useful information.

For the first time, Tennar took the 'pilot's chair' in the center of the compartment and strapped himself in — first the straps around his legs, just above the ankles, and then the seatbelt that came over his shoulders and buckled snuggly at the height of his sternum. There, he immediately fell into a deep sleep.

~

When he woke up, it became clear to Tennar that he had failed to dream. He felt certain, not that he couldn't remember the dreams he'd had, but that his mind had simply done no work at all while his eyes were closed. His face felt slack, his body as if it had been subjected to gravity. His bladder was giving him some discomfort, but it was by no means a desperate situation. And neither was his hunger. He could probably have remained in the chair another hour.

"Vessel?" he said and was relieved to see a scatter of light in response to this open-ended query. The lights trickled down the walls and into the floor, converging on Tennar's position in the chair. When they reached him, schematics brightened the monitor before him, and he watched Vessel show him something strange.

It appeared that the sensors had located a foreign object in the void around them. At first, Tennar thought Vessel had found an asteroid — some dead rock cast out of all gravitational auras. The ship's instruments had been unsuccessful at taking imagery of this object. It seemed capable only of capturing the contour of the form, which Vessel was using to render it out on the screen by means of a layering process that Tennar thought a bit technologically tedious.

By the time he recognized the object, his curiosity and hope had already sunk. "That's us, Vessel." Tennar nodded at the image Vessel had completed on the monitor. "That's the ship, you. All you did was find — "

But the ship had located another object. Lights jigsawed down the walls. Schematics blazed across the screen, and Vessel began forming the outline of the second object it had found, using the same method as before. Before it was finished, Tennar saw that it was the same object as before.

"That's still us. Probably, your sensors don't work in this place as they're supposed to. You're confused."

As he spoke, Vessel had alerted him to the presence of a third object, and the process repeated itself. Momentarily, Tennar entertained the notion that the ship was somehow being duplicated. But this was at the approximate apex of an ensuing collection of notions arranged in a hierarchy of bizarreness, through which he worked in descending order. By the time he made his mind's way to the most likely — being that Vessel was simply confounded by the existence of purely empty void — Vessel itself was making the eager discovery and outline of itself for the eighth time in a row.

Seeing this confusion as potentially endless — not unlike being lost within a hall of mirrors, yet somehow seeing oneself for the first time at every mirror — Tennar reached to unstrap himself from the chair with the idea of seeing to some of his basic needs. But he was paused by one last possibility — one that seemed to him still on that same hierarchy and in its proper order of plausibility: that Vessel was not confused but was attempting to communicate something to him that was true about their situation.

Assuming that Vessel knew it was locating itself in the void again and again was to conclude that it was trying to send Tennar a message: a message that couldn't be articulated by numbers and calculations and perhaps not even by words.

All at once, Tennar understood. The message that Vessel was sending him, in its simplest form, was this: "We are here." Repeated over and over the way a ship lost at sea repeats the same distress signal until it's picked up. What Tennar was made to understand by this was the astonishing fact that Nothing was no longer Nothing since he and Vessel were in it.

~

This was small comfort to Tennar, personally, but Vessel must have decided it had completed its mission. Tennar had found it easy to forget that their initial and far less logical purpose was to be a capsule of knowledge in the endless corridors of space and theoretical emptiness. This was the diametrical and less tenuous of the two functions that Vessel had performed. Having just recently destroyed their ability to return knowledge to humanity, this was what was left: to be a point of human somethingness within nothingness. Tennar supposed he was succeeding.

~

And yet: he sank into a deep despair. Tennar had not felt despair in a long time. He'd felt he was beyond it, that he should be. What could be causing it? He'd known he would not return to Gaia, and he'd surmised that he and Vessel would never arrive anywhere, which was essentially the same thing as arriving at nowhere. As he'd remarked to himself, very little about his situation had changed. So what had changed?

He'd unstrapped his legs from the pilot's chair before becoming distracted from his designs of using the facility compartment, and now he queried himself from a partially seated position, the seatbelt around his chest beginning to chafe a little.

Conversationally, Tennar asked himself, what was his problem?

34

The journey was over, and he knew he had left something un-
done or failed to accomplish something before its end. What was it? He
committed himself to the act of *thinking back*. The mind was a thinking
backward machine, moving backward (or inward, as the case may be) at
the same rate as Vessel's superlight relocations had been throwing them
forward in space.

In a sudden rage, just as suddenly spent, he slapped his hands
down on the arms of the chair, producing a short and measured applause
of echoes. The noise and agitation caused him to say it out loud: "What is
it?" he asked himself. "What did you want to accomplish?"

He thought back, relocating backwards at a monumental rate. It
was because of his belief in processes that had got him here, but the process had far more to do with the things that were unseen in the same way
that a life had much more to do with everything that couldn't be described
by that life's events. What he'd wanted to accomplish before the end of
his journey were memories. Not the memories that described what he'd
done or who he'd known or even those that would give him clues to who
he was. He wasn't interested in who he was, since who he was, for the
most part, couldn't be attributed to him.

He had been, was still (and now more than ever!) desirous of a
great accomplishment of memory; which, in some ways, had nothing to
do with him, personally. Or, to put it differently: he was chasing certain
memories that were beyond him and beyond knowledge — the failure to
know what they were or what they told him about himself being essential

to what they were and to their importance.

Tennar wasn't sure if the memory of the painting was one such memory. It was an image, certainly. Beautiful and strange (these words having absolutely nothing to do with how he felt about the memory of the painting, though they described the painting, the feeling, the memory as adequately as language would allow). But he felt that he had approached it with more frequency than it could sustain, and that it had been overtaken by imagination, and was in the process of dissolving.

Some part of his mind, then, told him that the type of memory he was asking for was impossible, that it couldn't be accomplished or contained. These memories that were like capsules of his soul sailing through the space of the mind, to be glimpsed like shooting stars. An awful flash of light, just as awfully brief.

And this impossibility, this insurmountability — more than the thought of the vast Nothingness surrounding him — contributed to his despair that gave rise to the long groan that escaped his lips.

~

Such a groan must have held enough intent to produce a conscientious query light from Vessel, which lowered itself down the wall to a level with Tennar's distant gaze like a spider on a gossamer strand of web. Tennar's eyes focused on the light, and he scowled at it.

"What good are you, then?" he asked it, to which it glowed a little brighter and settled back down to its original state.

Earlier in his journey, Tennar had experimented more frequently with Vessel's protocols, testing out its limitations of response and action. He had some control over its basic functions. He knew he even had some say in the ship's frequency of relocation and direction, but Tennar had avoided those sorts of commands since before their departure from the Milky Way galaxy. Vessel was programmed to accomplish its mission, if it could, which it had. Its only other protocol, that Tennar knew of, was in keeping him alive and comfortable — and this, only because keeping Tennar alive and comfortable was an unavoidable byproduct of Tennar's purpose: that of being a living human in the distant reaches of space.

The only aspect of the ship that didn't obviously line up with these two objectives were the two locked doors at its axes.

But now the conditions had changed.

Vessel, having fulfilled its first order of business, might have a new set of rules. Such was Tennar's reasoning. If he knew anything about computers, it was that they were very organized.

"If you're good for anything, how about you open those doors," which suggestion Tennar made instantly after asking it what it was good for, since his thoughts were working very quickly toward what he felt must be useful conclusions.

For that same reason, he failed to notice that the single wink of the query light might have been taken as a sign of acquiescence.

~

Not that Tennar needed this sign, since, anyway, he now had a feeling welling up inside of him of absolute certainty. It was, for him, one of those absolutely certain moments: the culmination of many separate pieces of thought — separate images made up of collections of separate pieces (he thought these things about his thoughts) fitting together quite suddenly to form one single image. He could put it another way to himself by imagining that his thoughts were contrived of separate lines or routes that were in the process of meeting in the exact center of his mind, connecting.

And this had to be where the painting was — in the center of his mind — waiting for him to arrive. Of course it was the painting that resided in the center! And the key to the possibility of arrival was in the memory itself. Tennar had remembered his memory of the love of the painting. And it was this memory of love that must have been essential to the actual image.

Ever since he'd first had the memory of the painting (as if from nowhere!), there had also arisen in Tennar's mind the idea that he understood, without understanding what it was he understood. This was the accomplishment of feeling he'd been looking for! He sensed that something connected to or something about the painting was explanation enough for the vastness of space and also for the void of nothingness in which he found himself now.

He unstrapped the belt around his chest and rose from the pilot's chair in a manner not in keeping with the excitement he felt. Probably, this was because of his extreme caution toward that excitement. How could he be anything other than disappointed when he tried to explore further the paths he had created in his mind for the memory of the painting from his earliest childhood? If he moved with increasing speed along the corridor from the navigation node, it was only from the renewed insistence of his bladder.

~

Vessel's lights had followed him here, to the first of the locked doors, gathering as points of brightness from all corners of the ship, flowing down the curvature of the walls in rivulets. Together, they gave the impression of time operating in reverse. They seemed, collectively, like a representation of space, turning in on itself. Like an idea forming. They looked like drops of bright water that flowed intricately along the invisible paths of a warp in a glass windowpane — droplets of water, oxygen and hydrogen, filled with the pale, electric light of a metropolis beyond the half-obscured window where anything might be happening. They converged on the outline of the door, filling the space with light.

Tennar hung before it as he had in times past, both recent and distant. He was reminded that outside this ship's hull there was a great expanse of nothing and nowhere to go, but this thought had very little impression on him. It was true: he understood some things and not others. And Vessel's lights reminded him of everything, and of nothing at the same time.

With formality and firmness, he told Vessel he'd like to enter this room.

Vessel's lights began to fill the surface of the door. Slip across the threshold and enter the space that the door was, each separate expression

39

of light to its own point — a process that began gradually, lights of what it was increasingly difficult to think of as Vessel's 'sensors' finding their individual points on the plane of the door, some of them overlapping or nearly so, and at an increasing pace until Tennar could no longer attempt to follow the logic of lights filling the surface of a door; something beyond that was happening now; there had been some transformation in the design of the process itself, but it was too bright for Tennar to look at it directly, the door; every light converging on this rectangular point in the ship; this space through which a human (Tennar) might pass, head, feet, and shoulders; what must have been every node the ship had, every single one of Vessel's lights until it seemed that the door itself was one single shape of white light.

Tennar found that he could look at it again. After almost turning his face away, he hadn't needed to. The white space of the door seemed somehow flat and dead, the lights — or light — no longer brightening the surrounding space. By the slow motion that he was never able to fully still, being weightless, Tennar saw that what he was looking at was not a door of light at all but the white room beyond. Where the door had been, now there was only a door-shaped space.

~

Had he been able to step carefully and with solemnity into the room, he would have. Tennar felt that the situation called for it. But solemnity was challenging without the ingredient of gravity, and he had to aim himself instead at the threshold with a push from the nearest catch net. Stopping himself from sailing straight into the room required that he catch himself against the wall beside the opening, and to keep this full stop from turning into a rebound meant that he had to also throw one arm into the room and hug the wall. This done, his momentum halted, Tennar could then pull himself into the room headfirst.

~

It was a small room with no further doors. Entering, Tennar was able to gather in its details and the details of the room's single object in no time at all. There, the painting hung on the wall to his right. He recognized it effortlessly. The deep blue water of the lake surrounded by verdant and mist-garmented mountains that were gently shaped like the humps of a camel: a grey-blue sky in the upper quarter which reached down as far as the water in the middle where the mountains parted; and there, at that point, between sky and water: the black panel, rectangular in shape and without shade or shadow or any obvious explanation, as if the artist had wanted only to mar the landscape he'd created.

Since it was the water that Tennar's memory had first responded to, he sank his eyes into this, the largest portion of the painting. Studied the quality of the color, its 'deepness', as if to return to a space, a moment, that memory had afforded him. He was aware of himself attempting to make his eyes 'see the painting more deeply', without knowing what this meant.

Then he could hide it from himself no longer: he was disappoint-ed.

He hadn't wanted the real painting. Probably, he'd known this, but how could he have known that the real painting was here on the ship for him to avoid? And even if he'd known… *Even if I'd known*, he kept thinking, over and over, repeating the thought to himself without advancing toward any further articulation of what he meant. It seemed too certain, hanging here in this once-locked, dead-end room in a ship that had taken him so far from his home that his memories — certain memories — seemed sublime for existing at all at the end of such enormous distance. Seeing it now, being in its physical presence, was like seeing the picture on a completed puzzle: a picture that had been on the box all along.

To what extent, Tennar asked himself, was this painting simply a recreation of his memory of the painting? He had no idea how to answer that. And, behind this question, two facts impressed themselves.

The first was a banal accoutrement of his immediate disappointment: the painting was smaller than he remembered. Tennar almost laughed. Of course it was. How much smaller than himself had he been when he'd been before it last?

The second fact was a reminder, born from a sense of diminishing excitement and purpose: he was reminded that outside this ship's hull there was a great expanse of nothing and nowhere to go. And this time, such a fact left a deep impression on his soul.

~

He could float for hours and hours around the orbital bay of the ship, which open space he had likened variously to the spine of a great whale-beast (a circular whale-beast!), the exoskeleton of a monstrous and strange worm, a representation of the infinite, the orbital plane of his entire existence, able to creatively forget that he was in a spaceship in space, void, matterless motion for many spans of time which he'd once called days. He was able, sometimes, to perceive that he was aging, or to feel that he was dissolving. If he took liberties with the meaning of the word, he thought that maybe he had dissolved — dissolved and been recreated, reassembled through the auguries of his own memories. He looked for this sensation. Sought it out. A tingling in the mind like that of a limb that's fallen asleep. He likened his memories of the past to various prognostications of the future, reordered them into many separate compartments for his soul to enter and exit again at will. The soul, he thought, which, in the end, was probably as diffuse as the particles in the void, and maybe just as vast. As thin as reality was out here, he too felt himself stamped flat by realities overlapping. He likened his life to his death. And, since he imagined sometimes that he could, while dissolving, remember his death, he also likened his death to his life. An endless series of mirrors confronted him at each turning of the circle, and — not knowing where he began nor where he'd ended — he imagined himself slipping into that time called afterlife, out of which his mind came covered in the fluids of afterdeath, and from there groping up through the soil of another beforedeath, his hair soaked with the waters of secondbirth. Then, like so many of his ideas, the stream he was floating on became a cascade of words that satisfied him greatly before draining completely away. He'd been trying to carry a lake in the cupped palms of his hands and had found he couldn't contain it nor hold on to a single drop. And he reasoned (out of spite) that everything was a dream regardless of whether or not he was dreaming.

In reality — whichever reality this was, dream or no — Tennar knew himself to be entirely alone now. Whatever it had taken Vessel to open the door to the room with the painting had been too much for it. Or had been its last protocol. Though the ship still functioned in a static, life-supporting, minimalistic way, the lights and sensors of the respondent computers were gone. The navigation node was a dark, dead space. He'd visited it and been frightened irrationally by the figure of the pilot's chair in the center of the room — turned so malevolently away from him — and had fled. He was alone, and he knew that he had been alone ever since he'd entered the ship called Vessel, even though its lights had meant many things to him and had reminded him of many images he'd known on Gaia: a place he realized again (having forgotten many times before, repeatedly) that he did miss.

His solitude had brought him to this. The loneliness (of his soul, possibly) had a tremendous effect on the reality around him. How else to explain that the first locked room in the ship that had taken him here had contained nothing but the isolated memory of the painting? Tennar some-how felt that he was to blame for the existence of nothing. This isolation beyond isolation, beyond knowledge. Into which the only knowledge he could bring was of incomplete memories and unsatisfactory images. His certainty was completely gone, and he was afraid of the final door —

afraid of finding out that it remained locked and equally afraid of finding out that it stood unlocked. After the room which had presented to him the image of his memory of the painting, what further disappointment could there possibly be?

~

But if memory was often indistinguishable from imagination, then forgetfulness (the empty spaces between memory) might also become pollinated with the seeds of creativity. Because of his immense solitude — and because Tennar was tired of it, was a-dust with self-pity — he had been capable of imaginatively forgetting the context of the memory of the painting, to isolate it. By his restless fixation on it and precious loneliness, single it out and set it apart from the house, the sunlit wall on which it hung, the presence of his father who'd held him up to see it, and the sensation of love that had filled what else but his soul the way the Gaian sunlight had filled the colors of the painting itself.

This was a revelation, of sorts, which—as with most revelations, most dreams — he couldn't remember if he'd had before. Without his father, there was no memory of the painting, since Tennar himself had been too young and too little to bring it to eye-level. And it was not overselling it (Tennar laughed to himself in the spacious gloom, filled with the humor of his propensity for overdoing every separate thought) to say that without his father, there would have been no painting at all, since it was his father who'd bought it and hung it on the wall of their old house.

Elated, and emptied of any further ideas, he pushed himself soaring around the arc of the hangar toward the second of the two last doors. He'd been afraid of it and might have gone on being afraid of it for a variety of reasons, but now he knew that he needed to at least test its weight, place his palms against the surface and push. He had no mind beyond this singular determination, this one final exertion.

~

When he reached the door, it was dark—like the rest of the ship, absent of any sensor lights and situated behind an eclipse of shadow. In order to approach it, Tennar had to work his way along the outer wall where the catch net was and position himself just to one side of the door. Push off lightly from the net; so lightly, he was barely moving at all — motion which contained a depth of silence that occluded even the sound of his own heart. In this fashion, he stopped himself against the inner wall with a tap of the tip of a finger.

He'd moved so softly and fluidly that he managed to absorb the rebound from this contact with the inner wall and remain hovering at a slanted, head-first angle within reach of the last door. There was not enough light in the ship now to see it as more than a depression of shadow in the wall. If he found that it was locked, what would he decide to do? Tennar tried to think of something, scoop up some quantifiable image that might allow him to draw some conclusion that would have some bearing on his present situation. Then he tried not to laugh at himself, since laughter would probably send him backwards out of the wall's reach. Last room or no last room, the entire scope of his ideas seemed to have drained away, and he was left in the dark hull of a dead ship with the knowledge that God had left a portion of the universe uncreated for his own purposes and that he, Tennar, was inside of this creative void and unlikely ever to emerge once more. His father had picked him up and held him under the arms before the painting in the sun-bright house. He remembered this. He had this memory.

He dipped his hand into the shadow beside him, reaching for the door, expecting hard, smooth metal. But he wasn't close enough. The door was set back into its threshold deeper than he remembered. He extended himself slowly, uncoiling. The door must have been deeper . . .

Puzzled, Tennar brought his bent arm toward the corner of the wall where the door was inset. Pulled himself forward and braced himself, boot and hand, between the inset. Now that he was situated, it was just a matter of finding the . . . pressing forward through this dark corridor he didn't remember. In fact, it was an awful lot like any number of other corridors between bay and room, even, he discovered, bending at right angles once, twice — a tubular hallway that was beginning to seem to Tennar like an endless in-between space long before it had any right to. The fact was that he had made his way through the corridor beyond the absent locked door for no more than ten minutes before he was blinded by a light.

~

Senses flooded by sudden light, Tennar hid himself behind his hands. He'd been startled into a backward roll and would crash into the corridor wall now or seconds from now, and he curled into a ball, blind, hugging his head and waiting for impact.

Which arrived more softly than expected, against his back. His eyes opened, watering, but he could see that the surrounding light was coming from the ship. He'd found Vessel. Or, rather, he'd found whatever part of Vessel it was that communicated with him. Tennar let out an excited gasp of greeting: "Vessel!" he cried. He was met by a stirring vortex of sensor lights, and he had the momentary impression that he was falling. Then the vortex halted; Tennar really did fall.

He fell about two feet to the floor of the corridor and collapsed in a heap. A great weight pressed him down. For a long time, he was unable to move, barely to breathe. For a long time after that, he had the strength only to make minor adjustments of body: lifting his head produced a throbbing pain in his neck; his arms were frail and ungraceful. Gathering his knees underneath of him, settling his weight on them, rising to his feet to produce a swaying and uncertain stand — all this took an uncalculated amount of time during which Tennar's mind basked in a state of perfect shock.

Somehow, Vessel had created a condition of gravity. This last room — which had to have been deep within the core of the ship — must also have been in spin. Enough to supply the area with the centrifugal force necessary to imitate gravity…Tennar wasn't satisfied with this conclusion. Something was not right. But it took as much mental energy to stand and walk as it demanded of his body — so unused to weight was he. And, as he relearned how to walk (wondering why he wasn't simply crushed), his mind was challenged by the unusual display of Vessel's lights around him.

Though the lights had not vanished, the corridor around Tennar had darkened. The sensor lights had withdrawn somehow, and Tennar saw them as pinpoints of white which emitted no ray nor aura nor glow, and they seemed to him incredibly distant, as far from him as the constellations of stars he'd once gazed at from Gaia's surface. Tennar stumbled through darkness, pricked by the depthless astral vastness that had become of the corridor. Though he was walking, he could not detect the floor along which he moved. Instead, it appeared to have been replaced by that same darkness, pricked by the same distant sidereal lights. Looking back the way he'd come, Tennar saw more of the same, the endless night.

Fear grasped him and wouldn't let go. He'd taken an involuntary sidestep and now could not recall which direction he'd been headed before. What had once been a corridor, a clear path that led somewhere definite, was now nothing more nor less than the image of outer space on all sides.

I might find the pole star and at least know I'm heading north, Tennar reasoned to himself. What an absurdity! He was traveling through open night without surface or destination and might have been in any galaxy at all. But there was gravity. He had to remember that this was an optical illusion, and to prove this to himself — forcing his exhausted body into a posture of bravado — he bent over and knocked his fist against the hard surface of the corridor floor: the same surface that his feet were currently standing on.

Except that his fist found no surface but flung down instead, further than the level of his feet so that he overbalanced and fell headfirst, falling exactly the way anything falls when not weightless. When he arrived at the end of his fall it was to crash into a semi-hard surface that gave way around him and gulped him up. He couldn't breathe. A pressure took hold of his lungs and pressed in around his flailing body until his head broke away from the airlessness. Struggling and painful with confusion, Tennar found that he was immersed in water. He must have wandered without knowing it into the final room and fallen into a vat — perhaps a backup coolant bin.

He was cold. Treading water with limbs unconditioned by weightlessness. If he didn't find the rim and climb out soon, he knew he would drown. Kicking out, Tennar extended himself one direction and then the other, touching nothing but water and filling up with an expanding panic. No one could have helped, but he cried out, "Help me!" before his head submerged once more. He had the thought of kicking himself up from the base of the vat, but his legs found no base, and having wasted moments, energy, air, he swam toward the surface again in a fit of desperation. When he broke through the surface, he was sobbing uncontrollably, crying out for someone to help him, Vessel, anyone! He saw through the chaos of his own turning, briefly, a kind of violet light at a distance from him unimaginable, and there were rounded shadows below the violet that were darker, gigantic, and he suspected that now he would drown.

But at the moment that his arms and legs had no strength left of their own, Tennar felt himself grasped under the arms and lifted. He was lifted clear out of the water and set down on a hard surface. Gasping and shivering (he was very cold!), he tried to turn his face up to see who had saved him. There was no one. He was dreaming, drowning in an immense and intricate dream; he must have been . . . but for the weight of his body and the hardness of the surface beneath him that felt like stone and could not be stone.

~

When he sifted up into a solidifying consciousness, it was because of the bright light that filled the space beyond his closed eyelids. Tennar knew that he had woken at last and that Vessel was aiming its sensors at him, trying to get his attention for some purpose and that Tennar should open his eyes and accept whatever knowledge the ship had to give him.

But he was reluctant to. He must have slept more deeply than ever he could remember because his body felt pressed in on itself and tremendously heavy, and his back and head were in active pain. Pain that gradually became more animate. A groan escaped his lips. He tried to remember where might the dream he'd been dreaming have begun and what had happened before he'd started dreaming, and then he stopped trying to remember. His thoughts were tied in knots of unknowing; his knowledge was that he was in a state of deep discomfort and consuming uncertainty. His body was far too warm, and when he reached, with heavy arms, for the straps he must have buckled around his chest and legs, he found them, the straps, missing. Feeling around, his bed seemed awfully like a Gaian stone: hard, rough, as unforgiving as the hot light that burned his eyes when he tried to open them —

What had he just seen in the space of a half-blind eyeblink? Tennar lay very still, momentarily terrified by what his senses were retrieving for his mind — his mind laying out, from habit, the blueprint of an idea designed to comfort him (whether from dream or from reality, it didn't matter): he reminded himself that he had already been witness to the sundering of all knowledge and had himself been a participant in knowledge's ultimate end. Such a thought seemed to him…almost pious.

Tennar had this idea and desired to draw some conclusion from it that would have some bearing on his present situation. What was his situation? Every cell of his body was filled with discomfort and dread. His mind flitted pitifully through a stream of useless words he couldn't latch on to: solitary, limitless, inherent, dream, memory, love — !

He opened his eyes and simultaneously threw his hands up to his face, peering through his trembling fingers at the scene that confronted him. Sounds that his mind had declined to register filled him, smells: he was surrounded by dark, deep blue water — moving, majestic water, deepened and aglow by light that was sunlight because there, directly before him—over the ridges of those gentle mountains — was the impossible orb of the sun itself. The sun? He'd seen thousands of suns. Nonetheless, this was the sun, golden and irrevocable beyond magenta levees of clouds.

Looking at the sun must have caused a blind spot in his vision because below it, where the water receded between the mountains to meet the sky, was a black shape, empty of depth or tone. And implacable because, though he blinked at it, it didn't fade. And if he continued his rapid blinking it was only to clear his eyes of the tears that were filling them and running down his cheeks — tears born of nothing but the fact that he was utterly overwhelmed — overwhelmed in a way that was almost neutral in accordance with his sudden idea which was as neutral: that he knew where he was and that it was equally impossible to be where he was.

~

Not long after he climbed to his feet, Tennar realized that his body was acclimating to its own weight. What had been a burden that had nearly drowned him the night before felt now like a solidification: Tennar was here. He couldn't be anywhere else but here, regardless of whether here was contained by the ship that was contained by Nothingness or whether he had relocated entirely out of space and time or whether it didn't matter. In fact, the substance behind the idea of containers, of things residing within their proper context (as with the idea of knowledge itself) had drained utterly away.

He was HERE! Tennar had the surmounting sensation that he had finally arrived, that he had always been trying to come here; and perhaps it had been this way with him ever since he was a child, lifted under the arms by his father to peer into his future and his yearning.

Who had lifted him out of the water and saved him from drowning? He was filled with the desire to find this person, thank him. Yes,

Tennar wanted to thank this person who'd saved his life. The thought consumed him, and he laughed. That's exactly how he would greet the person when he found him: laughing, he'd shout, "Thank you!"

He felt that it wouldn't be such trouble now to swim. He was stronger already — his body standing comfortably in the gravitational weight and the wind. The sound of the water lapping against the stone where he stood. The smell of damp and pine. He saw a fish break the surface of the water not six feet from his rock, its silver body catching the sunlight, and Tennar's mind leapt in the same manner, catching some attractive sight, rising swiftly from its deep place and bursting into the light of a clear memory:

He was in his father's arms, held, nearly weightless by the ease of his father's gentle movements. His searching eyes had caught something sun-brightened and lucid on the wall, which his father had brought him level with. Color and texture that his eyes drank: a place he knew that he would someday find himself, when he was older, after everything and everyone was gone — but he might find them again there, in that place, and everything that had been forgotten would be remembered there; and, though there was knowledge and memory and the presence of that absence — the dark shape on the horizon — it would still be a final, a creative, a simplistic completeness.

Tennar got into the water and swam for the green shore.

About the Author

Andrew is an author who lives in Grand Rapids, Michigan, with his wife and twin boys. His short fiction has appeared in journals such as *The Collagist, Black Static, Exacting Clam* (forthcoming), *Space & Time Magazine*, and others, including the first two volumes of *Solum Journal*. This is his first published book. Connect with him on Twitter @DrewReichard.